Jake Maddox JV Girls books are published by
Stone Arch Books
a Capstone imprint
1710 Roe Crest Drive
North Mankato, Minnesota 56003

www.mycapstone.com

Copyright © 2018 Stone Arch Books

Cataloging-in-Publication Data is available on the Library of Congress website.
ISBN: 978-1-4965-5915-9 (library binding)
ISBN: 978-1-4965-5917-3 (paperback)
ISBN: 978-1-4965-5919-7 (eBook PDF)

Summary: Ana Flores has always been more interested in books than sports. But when the women's softball team at the local college piques her interest, she decides to give the sport a shot.

Designer: Lori Bye

Photo Credits: Shutterstock: Bryce Newell, cover, cluckva, 90-95, (background), Eky Studio, chapter openers (background), Evgenii Matrosov, back cover, chapter openers (baseball design)

Printed and bound in China.
1107

CATCHING
CONFIDENCE

BY JAKE MADDOX

text by
Sarah Hannah Gómez

STONE ARCH BOOKS
a capstone imprint

TABLE OF CONTENTS

CHAPTER 1
SOMETHING UNEXPECTED. **5**

CHAPTER 2
LOST. **11**

CHAPTER 3
AND FOUND! **17**

CHAPTER 4
BACK TO SCHOOL. **25**

CHAPTER 5
IN THE PARK **33**

CHAPTER 6
TRYOUTS **41**

CHAPTER 7
BATTER'S BOX **49**

CHAPTER 8
STATISTICIAN **57**

CHAPTER 9
THE FIRST GAME. **65**

CHAPTER 10
PRACTICING **71**

CHAPTER 11
IN A PINCH **77**

CHAPTER 12
A NEW SAGA **87**

SOMETHING UNEXPECTED

"Aha!" said the queen. "But that's not who I am. I am —"

Drip! A glob of peanut butter landed right in the middle of the page that Ana Flores was reading. "Argh!" Ana said out loud.

She looked in her lunch bag for a napkin. She needed to wipe the peanut butter off in a hurry so she could find out what happened next.

She held her sandwich in her left hand and used her left elbow to hold the book open.

Then she swiped her napkin across the page with her right hand. It left a brown streak, but at least she could see the words again.

Two sentences later, she dripped another big glob onto the book.

"Argh!" Ana said again. After wiping the book clean, she set it down on the grass by her feet. Eating without a plate or a table was hard enough without trying to read at the same time. She would have to wait to finish her book until after she was done eating lunch.

She took a big gulp of water from her turquoise bottle as she looked around her. It was beautiful out, crisp and chilly but not too cold. Ana and her mom had just moved to the Southwest that fall. Though Ana missed her old friends, she was happy about the weather. It was January, and all she was wearing was a light jacket. The sun was shining. There were still three more days before school started again after the winter break.

When she finished eating, Ana took another napkin from her lunch bag. She carefully poured some water from her bottle onto it. Then she used the wet napkin to wipe all the peanut butter and honey off her hands.

Usually after lunch she went straight back to her mom's office, but it was so nice outside today. She wanted to stay out as long as possible.

As she walked, Ana thought about the book she was reading. It was part of her favorite series, and she was dying to find out what would happen now that the queen had been revealed as an imposter.

She was walking by a chain-link fence when she heard a cracking noise. Then there was another one, this time followed by a yell. Ana couldn't hear what the person said.

She kept walking along the fence until she came to a gate. She stopped there for a moment, listening to the cracks and the voices.

Ana really wanted to know what was happening. She couldn't see anything from where she was standing. There was a building in her way. It was definitely an open area of some kind, but she couldn't see any of the people she was hearing.

She really wanted to go in. *I could always just say I got lost if I get in trouble,* she reasoned. *Nobody would be mean about that. I'm a 12-year-old girl!*

Ana carefully opened the gate just wide enough so she could slide through. She held on to the gate so it would close without slamming. It squeaked, and Ana hoped no one had heard it.

She walked toward the building that had been in her way. She came to another fence that separated the bleachers behind her and a baseball field in front of her. Putting her things down, she went right up to the fence, pressing into it so she could get as close as possible to the action.

The voices she had heard were spread all over the field — twenty or so girls in uniforms.

A few of them were throwing and catching balls. The rest were lined up by home plate, taking turns hitting. Not a baseball field, then. Softball. The university's softball team was practicing.

Ana watched, amazed. Every girl who came up to bat hit the ball far across the field. No one ever missed. It began to feel almost like music and dance. Someone stepped up to the plate. The pitcher wound up and threw. The ball hit the bat with a crack and then, even though she knew she was imagining it, Ana could almost hear the ball soar through the air and land with a satisfying little *thump* in somebody's mitt. She couldn't take her eyes away.

Ana's phone buzzed in her pocket. It was a text from her mom that said:

Almost ready to go. Where are you?

Oops! She was late. Ana quietly walked back to the gate where she'd let herself in. Once she had closed it, she ran back the way she had come.

CHAPTER 2

LOST...

"Whew!" Ana's mother said as they walked to her car. "I think my office is finally clean enough for students to come in and meet with me."

"Good thing they aren't coming over to our house, Mami," Ana said jokingly. "That's never clean enough."

Her mother laughed and poked her in the side.

Ana's mother, Dr. Lucia Flores, was a college professor. She and Ana had moved to town for her job at Southwest University.

Ana loved coming to campus with her mom and seeing everyone walk around with heavy backpacks full of books. She imagined that everybody on a college campus must love reading as much as she did.

Mami started up the car, and they pulled out of the parking lot. "So where did you disappear to?" she asked Ana. "Were you off reading your book somewhere?"

"Yes! Mami, you will never believe the twist that happened!" Ana leaned forward and reached for her backpack. She unzipped it, but the book wasn't in there.

Just to be absolutely sure, she opened some of the smaller pockets, even though it was impossible for a book to fit into them. It wasn't there.

Ana thought for a moment and remembered putting her things down on the bleachers while she watched the softball practice. She hung her head. *I can't believe I left the book there!* she thought.

By now, her mother was listening to the news on the radio and hadn't noticed that Ana was worried about something.

"Mami?" Ana asked.

"Yes?"

"Are we coming back tomorrow?"

Her mom looked at her. "Well, I have to, but if you don't want to I suppose we can try to arrange something."

"No, I want to . . . I want to check out the library," said Ana. "I've only been in there once or twice, and it's huge."

"OK, great. Then we'll both be going to work tomorrow," Mami joked.

Ana sighed with relief. No one would steal a book from a softball stadium, would they? And this way she'd have another chance to watch the team practice!

***

After dinner, Ana went to her usual spot in the living room — a bright purple, lumpy old loveseat. She settled in, only to remember that she didn't have her book! She was so desperate to find out what happened next, and now she would have to wait until tomorrow — assuming her book was still on the bleachers.

She hated that she had lost her book, but watching the softball players practice had been pretty cool. Maybe even worth it.

"Hey, Mami?" Ana said. Mami was lying on the couch with a magazine. Their house was always quiet at night since they both read so much.

"Hmm?"

"Can I borrow your tablet?" Anna asked.

"Sure. It's in my room," Mami replied.

Ana got her mother's tablet and brought it into her room. Opening up an Internet browser tab, she typed *Southwest University softball* into the search engine.

Pages and pages of results popped up. She tapped the first one and was taken to the university's own website for their athletics department. She read about their wins and losses from last season and then clicked on *Roster*. For each person on the team, there was a photo, jersey number, position, and a bio. Her heart was racing.

Ana clicked and clicked. When she had read everything on the university's website, she went back to her search results and read more and more. It wasn't until her mom came and tapped her on her shoulder that she realized she had fallen asleep watching a video of the university's star hitter.

She changed into her pajamas, but not before saving all the tabs as favorites so that she'd be able to find them again.

AND FOUND!

As soon as they arrived on campus the next day, Ana rushed out of the car. "Going to the library?" Mami asked. "You're so antsy! Just remember that it's not like the public library. A lot of the books are for studying, so it won't just be a room full of Ana-approved fantasy adventures."

"I know, Mami!" Ana said, avoiding saying yes to her question. She didn't want to lie to her mother, but she also didn't want to tell her she had lost her brand new book.

And anyway, she could go to the library *after* she got the book from the softball stadium, and then it wouldn't be a fib.

"Make sure you have your phone in case I need to contact you," Mami said. It was her way of saying goodbye.

"I have it!" Ana said. She dashed out of the parking lot and raced toward the softball stadium.

She found the softball field quickly. Luckily, the gate was open again today. She could hear the sounds of practice again. Ana slipped in and went back to the bleachers where she'd been the day before.

No book.

Ana sighed. She blinked rapidly, not wanting to cry. First she had dripped peanut butter all over the pages. Now she would have to tell her mother that she lost a book after saving her allowance to buy it.

"Is this yours?" said a voice behind her.

Ana jumped. She turned around and saw a young woman in a softball uniform standing behind her . . . holding Ana's book!

"Yes!" Ana said.

The girl came closer. "I saw it yesterday after practice. It looked . . ." she looked down at the book, which had peanut-buttery fingerprints on the cover in addition to the stained pages. "It looked well loved, so I thought I should take care of it."

"I forgot it here," Ana explained. She took the book from the young woman. "My mom texted and I got distracted."

"You were watching us practice?" asked the softball player.

"Yeah!" Ana said, with a grin. "You guys are amazing."

"Thanks," the girl said. She stuck out her hand. "I'm Caitlin. I'm one of the pitchers." They shook hands.

"How'd you get on the team? Are there tryouts for the whole university?" Ana asked. Ana talked very fast when she was excited about meeting new people.

Caitlin smiled. "No, in college you get recruited. Coaches visit high schools and watch us play. Then, if we're lucky, they offer us spots on their teams. We get a scholarship for school and we get to play the entire time we're students."

Ana knew from her research last night that Southwest U had one of the top softball teams in the country. *Caitlin must be really good,* she thought.

"Hey," Caitlin said. "Want to come down and watch us practice?"

Ana nodded excitedly. "I'd love to!"

She followed Caitlin around the stadium. There were a few people in bleacher seats also watching. Two people, a girl about Ana's age and her dad, glanced at Caitlin and Ana.

The girl had dark, almost-black hair and a broad nose. She looked Ana right in the eye as she walked by. Ana couldn't tell if she was angry at her or jealous. She turned her head away and continued following Caitlin to the team's dugout.

Caitlin pointed to a bench where a few other softball players sat. "Make yourself at home," she said. Shyly, Ana sat at the very edge of the bench.

"Who's your friend, Caitlin?" one of the other softball players asked.

"Oh! I didn't actually catch your name," Caitlin said.

"It's Ana," Ana said.

"Nice to meet you," the other athlete said. "I'm Shanice."

"She plays center field," Caitlin said.

Ana recognized Shanice from her research last night. Shanice was famous for how high she could jump when catching a fly ball. She had kept a lot of opposing teams from getting home runs.

Caitlin was pulling her long, curly hair into a ponytail, and then she put her visor on. "Time to warm up," she said. "Enjoy, Ana! If you have any questions, ask Niran over there. He always knows what's going on. It's his job!"

Niran, a guy who seemed about the same age as Caitlin and Shanice, looked over from the other end of the dugout and gave her a nod. Ana nodded back.

Caitlin and Shanice ran out to the field to join their teammates. In four lines, the team began warming up, hopping, shuffling, and bending up and down to stretch their muscles. When they were far away, it was harder to figure out who was who, and she lost track of Shanice. Caitlin's jersey said *JONES* on the back and had the number 42.

Ana felt someone sit down next to her. Turning to look, she saw Niran.

"So what do you do for the team?" Ana asked.

"I'm the statistician," he said. "It's my job to make note of each player's stats — hits, pitches, that sort of stuff."

"Wow!" Ana said. "That's a lot."

"It's still pre-season," he said. "So you won't catch them doing anything too exciting. Do you play softball?"

Ana shook her head. "I just like watching," she said. She didn't want to explain that she had only been interested in softball since yesterday.

"You should try playing, then," Niran said. "What grade are you in?"

"Seventh."

"My little sister's in seventh too. She loves softball." He tilted his head up, as if he was trying to point to something in the bleachers. "Definitely give it a try."

Ana nodded. "Maybe," she said. She sat back to watch the action.

CHAPTER 4

BACK TO SCHOOL

It was lunchtime on the first day back to school after winter break. Ana was waiting to pay for her lunch and saw her friend Cara Mayfield waving to her from a table. As soon as Ana was finished in line, she rushed over.

"Did you read it? Did you read it?" Cara said breathlessly.

Ana knew exactly what she was talking about. Both of them were positively obsessed with the Endless Saga fantasy book series.

Once Ana had gotten her book back from Caitlin, she read the rest of it that same day. Then she read it all over again.

"Twice!" she told Cara proudly. "And I want to read it again!"

"Me too!" Cara said. "And guess what I heard!"

"What?" Ana asked.

"Even though the series isn't done yet, they re-released the first book — as a comic! I saw it at the bookstore the other day."

Ana squealed. "That is so cool! I would love to see what all the characters look like."

"I know!" Cara said. "I can't wait to get it."

"What did you do over the break?" Ana asked her friend.

"Read mostly," said Cara. "My parents worked most of break, so we didn't do anything special."

"Oh, sorry," Ana said. She was lucky that her mom had school breaks just like Ana did, so they could spend time together.

"It's OK," Cara said. "The babies still had daycare, so I got the house to myself!" Cara had two much younger sisters, and sometimes they drove her crazy. The Mayfield house was not very big, so Cara really appreciated her alone time. She loved going over to Ana's house, where it was just two people in the entire house.

"That's nice," Ana said. She felt bad. It had been so nice to spend time with her mother, it hadn't even occurred to her to call Cara much while school was out. Cara had been her first friend when she moved out here. *I should have been more thoughtful,* Ana thought.

"You know, you could have come over to hang out," she said. "I just assumed you were spending time with your family."

"Thanks," Cara said. "Next time."

Ana got the feeling that even though Cara lived in a crowded house with lots of family, she felt lonely sometimes.

"Anyway," Cara said, "maybe this weekend we can read the comic together. It comes out on Friday. My mom said she would take me to the mall after school to buy it."

"Awesome!" said Ana. "I'll ask my mom too."

Cara grinned at her. They spent the rest of lunch talking about the big twist in the book and what it might mean for the next book in the series.

***

On Saturday, Ana begged her mom to take her to the bookstore. It didn't take much convincing. "Your grades were great last semester, and I know seventh grade can be tough — especially when you've just moved to a new town. I think you deserve a treat!" Mami said.

They drove to the big mall in the center of town. Usually they headed straight for the bookstore, but this time they took their time peeking into other stores as well.

Mami picked up a new bottle of the fancy hair product she used, and they shared a cinnamon bun in the food court. Finally they headed for the bookstore.

In the window of the store was a gigantic cardboard cutout of the cover of the Endless Saga comic book. Ana could barely contain her excitement.

She walked over to the garbage can to throw away the cinnamon bun wrapper and looked to her left. Next to the bookstore was a sign that said, *ATHLETICS HUB: SPORTS SUPPLIES FOR GIRLS AND BOYS.*

Mami walked up behind Ana and put her hand on her shoulder. "Well? I can't believe you're not running in there to get your book."

Ana looked up at her mom. "Mami? I think there's something else I want for my treat instead."

***

"You didn't get the book?" Cara shouted. Thankfully the cafeteria was already noisy, so nobody looked their way.

Ana shrugged. "I really want to read it," she said. "But I decided to get something else instead. Anyway, can't I borrow your copy when you're done?"

Cara's face fell. "Ellie fell down and broke her arm on Thursday. My dad said the medical bills are going to be high, so we can't afford extras for a while," she said. "I wanted to borrow the comic from you when *you* were done!"

"Oh, Cara," Ana said. "I had no idea. I'm sorry!"

Cara gave a weak smile. Ana could tell she was forcing herself to do it, even though she was upset. "It's OK. You didn't know."

"We'll have to try the school library *and* the public library," Ana suggested. "One of them has to have it. We can read it together, like we said we would."

"OK," Cara said. She hunched forward and looked down at her feet. "I guess that's what we'll have to do."

***

Later that day, Ana came home from school and went straight to her room. Lying on her desk was the treat her mom had gotten her. She picked it up and hugged it to herself. She was sad that she didn't get to read the comic book yet, but not too sad — because in her arms was a beautiful new softball glove and a bright green softball.

CHAPTER 5

IN THE PARK

Ana was done with her homework for the weekend, so she decided to spend the rest of her Sunday afternoon reading at the park. Usually the park was quiet, but when she arrived today she heard commotion. As she approached, she saw three people in a big clearing . . . playing softball!

Ana watched as two girls her age, plus an older man, ran some kind of drill. The man would throw the softball so that it stayed low and bounced or rolled on the ground.

One girl, short with dark brown hair, would crouch, dive, or bend over to catch it, and then quickly swivel to throw it overhand to the second girl who was waiting far behind her. That girl, who was much taller, threw it to the man, and then it started again.

Ana settled on a bench that kept her near the action without being too close. She watched as the girl caught every single one of the man's throws, no matter how much he tried to trick her by throwing it in a different direction or lower to the ground. She zipped around so fast and with such precision that Ana was astonished.

The other girl was good too. She didn't seem as comfortable as the brown-haired girl, but she caught most of the balls and had a good throw.

Ana looked closely. The dark-haired girl and the man looked familiar.

They're the ones I keep seeing at practices! she realized.

They were always sitting in the front row of the bleachers when Ana would walk past them to meet Caitlin and Niran in the dugout. No wonder the girl was so good. She must have been really into softball.

Soon the man yelled, "Great, girls! Now switch places." The two girls ran past each other, giving each other a high five as they went.

They went two rounds before the girl in back threw the ball way over the man's head. It landed just to the left of Ana's bench.

All three turned to look at her. She stared back for a moment, confused. *The ball!* she thought to herself. She scrambled to get up, but by then the tall girl was already at the bench with her, retrieving the softball.

"Got it!" she shouted. She raised her arm to throw it back, but the man stopped her.

"Let's take a quick break and get some water," he suggested.

The girls grabbed water bottles and chugged large gulps. The man gestured to Ana. "Come on over," he called to her. She hesitated for a moment, then got up and walked over.

"I'm Kiet Kunchai," he said. "This is my daughter Mali and her friend Laura." Laura smiled.

Before Ana could introduce herself, Mali jumped in. "*Daaaaad,*" she whined. "We've seen her at SU practices. She's always in the dugout."

Mr. Kunchai peered more closely at Ana. "That's right! We have. And your name is?"

"Ana," she said. "Nice to meet you."

"So you must play softball," he said.

"Umm . . . ," Ana started to say.

"You should play with us!" he said. "Do you live nearby? Run get your glove, then join us."

"Really?" Ana said hesitantly.

The man grinned. "Sure! We'll be here. Go on and get your stuff so you can join in."

"It'll be fun!" said Laura.

"Um . . . OK," Ana said. "I'll be right back."

***

Walking back to the park, Ana suddenly felt awkward. Watching softball was one thing. Playing was another. *But this is my chance to try,* she thought.

"Hey, Ana," Laura called as Ana approached. "We decided just to play catch for a while." She tossed the ball underhand to Ana.

Ana couldn't get her glove on in time. She tried to catch the ball with her bare hand but missed it.

"Sorry!" Laura giggled. "I didn't realize you didn't have your glove on yet."

"It's OK," Ana said. She picked up the ball and tossed it back, then put her glove on her left hand. She hadn't worn it much, so it was very stiff.

Ana stepped into the circle. Laura threw the ball to Mali, who threw it to her dad. Mr. Kunchai lobbed it at Ana. She held her glove out like a scoop. The ball bounced out.

She picked it up from the ground and threw it overhand to Laura. Leaping forward, Laura tried to catch it before it landed a few feet short.

"Sorry," Ana said quietly.

"No problem!" Laura said. "It happens."

Around in a circle they went, tossing the ball to the person next to them. Then Mr. Kunchai reversed the direction. Mali wound up and pitched the ball to Ana, hard. Instinctively, Ana jumped out of the way. The ball rolled past her.

"Nice," Mali said sarcastically.

"Mali!" Mr. Kunchai said. "Better luck next time, Ana."

Ana sighed. Mali didn't seem to want her there, but at least Laura and Mr. Kunchai were nice to her.

Mr. Kunchai gave Ana tips on how to hold her glove when a ball was coming from high or low. A half hour later, Ana was catching most of the balls thrown her way.

After a bit longer, Mr. Kunchai looked at his watch. "That's long enough. We gotta pack it in."

"Aww," Ana said. She hadn't realized she was having so much fun.

Laura jogged over to her. "Good job, Ana. You go to City Junior High, right? You looked familiar."

"Yeah!" Ana said.

"Are you going to try out for the softball team?" Laura asked.

"There's a softball team?" Ana asked. Her old school had lost money for sports, so the last time she had played was first grade, which really didn't count.

"Of course! Tryouts are tomorrow after school. See you there, I hope!" Laura ran off to join Mali and Mr. Kunchai. He waved at her kindly, while Mali waved with an expression that was neither a smile nor a frown.

Hmm, Ana thought to herself. *Maybe I should go for it.*

CHAPTER 6

TRYOUTS

After school the next day, Ana rushed to her locker to get her phone. She checked her email. Last night she had emailed Caitlin to ask for advice on tryouts.

Caitlin had replied!

You should definitely try out for the team! You'll learn a lot and it will be a great way to meet more people since you're still pretty new in town. Don't expect to be the star right away, but do your best!

Ana smiled to herself. Inside her backpack were workout clothes and her softball glove. After changing in the bathroom, she headed out to the field.

***

About thirty girls were outside. Ana wondered how many were eighth graders who had been on the team last year and how many were seventh graders like she was.

She put her hands up to shield her eyes from the sun and looked for Laura and Mali. They were standing with a few other girls. Ana walked up to them. *I hope Laura really meant that I should try out. This will be awkward if she didn't really want me to come,* she thought.

"Ana!" Laura said cheerfully. "You came! You decided to try out!"

Ana nodded.

"Hey," Mali said.

"Everyone, this is Ana," Laura said. "Ana, this is . . . everyone." The other four girls in the group introduced themselves.

Ana stood silently while everyone chattered about who they thought would make the team. "There are so many eighth graders here I bet none of us will make it," a girl named Shireen said.

Mali shook her head. "That's not fair. They have to take the best players. Just because someone is older doesn't mean they deserve to make the team more than we do."

"That's not very nice, Mali," Shireen said. But before she could say more, a whistle blew.

"Bring it in, ladies!" a woman called. Everyone ran over to circle around her.

"Hi, everyone," the woman said. She had warm brown skin and an even warmer smile. "For those of you who don't know me, I'm Coach Robinson. Welcome to softball tryouts! I'm glad you're here."

Some girls cheered. Coach Robinson smiled at them. Girls began passing around name tags and pens. Ana wrote her name on one and stuck it to her shirt.

"OK, here's what's going to happen," she said. "These young women to my right are Nadia, our starting batter, and Kay, our second baseman. They will lead you in warmups. Then we'll divide into groups to test your fielding and hitting. Remember softball is a team sport. You should all be helping each other to look good as well, not getting in each other's way or making a bad throw. Ready? Everyone find a spot on the field to warm up."

Everyone turned and spread out.

"OK, everyone!" Nadia yelled across the field. "High knees!"

Ana and a few girls looked around in confusion. When everyone else began running in place, getting their knees up as high as they could and close to their chests, Ana did the same.

A few moments later, Kay yelled, "Touch your heels!" Now everyone kicked their feet behind them while running in place, tapping their heels as they came up behind them.

Next, Nadia shouted, "Jumping jacks!" All the girls on the field jumped in unison. "A little faster when you can!" she added.

They went on that way until Coach was satisfied. "OK, everyone!" she called. "If you're on my right, get your gloves and follow Nadia to the outfield. If you don't have a glove, there are some in the dugout you can use for today. If you're on my left, come with me and Kay to home plate."

The groups separated. Laura headed toward home plate. Ana grabbed her glove and went out to the field. She noticed Mali was in her group. She wished it was Laura instead.

Ana stayed to the back of the group while Nadia explained what they would be doing. "We're going to start with grounders," she said.

"I'll throw them. You catch and throw it back to me as fast as you can. Each of you will get three, then the next girl will go. We'll do two rounds. Got it?"

Everyone nodded. Nadia was all business. They lined up, and somehow Ana ended up in front. She walked up to face Nadia. "Here's your first one," Nadia called.

The ball came rolling toward Ana so fast, she barely had time to put her glove on. The ball went right through her feet. She was shocked they had started so fast. She thought Nadia might want to ask her name or something. Or give her a little warning, at least.

"Sorry!" she called.

She ran and picked up the ball, then threw it back to Nadia. When Nadia immediately threw it back, Ana was ready. She spread her legs into a V, set her glove on the ground, and scooped up the ball.

They continued on for a couple more rounds. On the Nadia's last throw to Ana, the last ball bounced right over her glove. But Ana reacted quickly, retrieved the ball, and threw it back to Nadia.

Nadia's face was expressionless. "Next!" she called.

Ana watched everyone else closely. She wanted to see their technique, and she also wanted to know if everyone was more experienced at softball than she was. A few girls looked like they hadn't played before either. Or maybe like Ana, they hadn't played since elementary school.

Soon it was Ana's turn again. She caught all three of Nadia's balls this time, but one of the ones she threw back went far over Nadia's head. As she followed it with her eyes, she saw Coach standing nearby, watching. Ana hung her head. *That probably ruined my chances,* she thought. *Maybe I shouldn't even stay for the rest of tryouts.*

CHAPTER 7

BATTER'S BOX

The whistle blew. "Time to switch!" called Coach Robinson.

Ana followed her group to the infield. They gathered around home plate to hear what they were doing next.

"OK, everyone. Now I want to see your hitting, pitching, and catching." Coach explained, "Everyone is going to try batting, but if you want to focus on only pitching or only catching rather than both, that's fine."

"You're going to bat first," she went on. "Line up back there. I'll be pitching to you and Kay will be my catcher. You'll each get three swings."

This time, Ana was in the middle of the line. The first girl up to bat hit a line drive on her first try with a loud crack. It flew past Coach Robinson and into the outfield.

"Great!" said Coach. She picked up another ball from the pile on the mound and pitched again. The girl didn't swing. "Good eye! Too high." The third one she hit, and Coach caught it easily.

"Great job," Coach said to the girl. "Next!"

The next girl had been behind Ana in line during their fielding tryout. She caught every ball Nadia threw at her, but she wasn't as good at batting. She got two strikes and hit a fly ball on her third swing.

When it was Ana's turn she picked up the bat and grasped it low. She was already nervous, and now the bat shook.

"Choke up a little," Coach suggested. Ana moved her hands a bit higher on the bat. "Good."

She threw the first pitch. Ana watched it carefully. She had figured out from watching the other girls that sometimes Coach threw a ball too high or too low on purpose to see if they'd know not to swing. Finally the ball looked good, but it was too late. It was in Kay's mitt. Ana had waited too long to swing.

"Strike!"

Coach pitched again. Ana swung fast before the ball was close enough. "Strike!"

Ana sighed. *I have to get* one, *right? Everyone so far has hit at least one.* She looked hard at Coach's arm and watched the entire windup. She concentrated and swung.

There was a tiny cracking sound. The ball bounced off her bat and fell to the ground.

Ana shrugged and handed the bat off to the next girl. *Was that good enough?* she wondered.

When Mali's turn came, she strode up to the plate with confidence. Coach seemed to be familiar with her. She wound up and pitched harder than she had to some of the other girls. Mali swung and hit a fly ball. On her second, she hit a grounder. On the third, she swung hard at a perfect pitch . . . and didn't hit the ball.

Mali threw the bat off to the side and walked off. Everyone stared. The mood on the infield changed.

After the last girl had her turn, Coach ran out to the field to check on the other group. Kay turned and spoke to Ana's group. "OK, everyone. If you're interested in pitching, head up to the mound. If not, you're playing catcher."

Mali made a beeline for the pitcher's mound. Everyone separated. Ana was left. "Well?" Kay asked.

Ana thought for a moment. She was new, but what did that matter? Caitlin was a pitcher, so maybe Ana could be one too. "I'll try pitching," she said.

"Great," Kay said.

Ana joined the five girls brave enough to stand at the pitcher's mound. Each of them was going to pitch once to each girl playing catcher. That was it. That meant Ana only had to pitch seven balls. She was sure she could do that.

"Who's first?" Kay asked. Mali raised her hand. *Of course,* thought Ana.

The first catcher crouched down behind the plate. Then Kay stepped in with a bat.

Mali wound up and threw the ball straight down the middle. Kay hit a line drive with no problem. "Great," she said. "Next." Another pitcher stepped up. Kay hit her ball too.

Ana was last. She took a deep breath, determined not to let her nerves get the best of her. *You can do this,* she told herself. *Anybody can throw a softball.* She wound up and threw.

The ball went high as if someone had just hit a pop fly. The catcher jumped up and caught it.

"Whoa," said Kay. "Calm down there, tiger." Ana felt her cheeks burning. Kay turned to the catcher and added, "Good job, though."

The catchers switched out and everyone started again. Ana noticed that Coach was back from the outfield, watching from a distance. On her second try, Ana nearly hit Kay. "Watch it!" Kay said sharply.

On her third try, Ana didn't go too high or outside. Kay hit the ball easily. "Better," she said, "but you stepped over the line." Ana looked down. She hadn't been paying attention to the line on the mound at all. It was enough just to concentrate on throwing the ball properly.

By the end, Ana had thrown two pitches that Kay could actually hit, and the rest were all over the place. *At least the catchers are getting exercise,* she thought bitterly.

Coach blew the whistle. "Bring it in!" The outfielders ran in, shouting excitedly. Coach blew the whistle again to get everyone to quiet down. "Great work today, everyone. I'm happy all of you came. The team list will be posted by the gym tomorrow by lunchtime. Have a great night!"

Everyone cheered.

CHAPTER 8

STATISTICIAN

The next day at lunchtime, Ana waited to meet up with Cara. She wanted her friend with her when she checked the team list. Even though Cara wasn't interested in softball, Ana knew Cara would be excited for her.

"Hey!" both girls said at the same time when they saw each other. "Guess what!"

They laughed. "You go first," Ana said.

Cara pulled something out of her backpack. It was the Endless Saga comic book!

"My mom and dad said I have been so helpful with my sisters that I deserved a treat. Isn't it beautiful? I thought we could go to the library after we eat and read it together."

Ana's heart sank. She was so excited to read the book, but her stomach was doing butterflies thinking about the softball team. "Before we do that, can we stop by the gym? I want to see if I made the softball team."

"Softball?" Cara said. "Since when do you play softball?"

"Since . . . yesterday, I guess," said Ana. "I mean, I already liked it, but at the last minute I decided to go to tryouts."

Cara frowned.

"What?" said Ana.

"I don't know," Cara said. "I just never thought of you as a sports person. You're a book person, like me."

Ana shrugged. "Maybe I'm both."

Cara looked at her strangely. "Well, I guess we can go look at the list and then go to the library. We just can't take too long. I kept myself from reading this all last night so I could share it with you."

The girls ate in a hurry. They threw their garbage in the trash and compost and then rushed over to the gym. There were two pieces of paper posted on the door. Other girls were crowded around them. Cara stayed back, while Ana pushed her way forward to read them.

The one on the left said *VARSITY*. Ten names were on it. The second said *JUNIOR VARSITY*. Another ten names were there. Each team had one extra person as an alternate. Ana read both quickly. Then she read them again more slowly. Then she read them one more time.

Her name wasn't on either list.

She hung her head and walked back to where Cara stood. "I didn't make it," she said.

"No big deal, right?" Cara said. "I mean, you've never talked about softball before."

Ana didn't know how to explain it. Even though she hadn't played softball since she was a little kid, she had been excited to discover the U's team. She loved watching the action and seeing how powerful and happy everyone on the team seemed to feel. *Maybe I'm just meant to be a spectator, not a player,* she thought.

Cara turned to walk away just as the door to the gym opened.

"Ana!" someone called. "I'm glad I caught you." It was Coach Robinson. Ana came closer.

"Ana, I'm sorry I didn't have room for you on the team this year, but I can tell you're really passionate about the sport." Ana nodded. "I noticed you are very observant and careful about things. I thought maybe you would want to help me out on the junior varsity team and be our statistician."

Like Niran! Ana thought.

"You would come to all our practices and games and take notes. Write down everyone's scores and plays, that sort of thing," Coach explained. "And I might need your help with other things now and again. Are you interested? You'd be an honorary Lion."

Ana thought for a moment. She really wanted to be on the team, and this seemed like her chance. Being statistician wouldn't be anywhere near as exciting as playing, but it was better than nothing.

"OK," she said.

"Wonderful!" Coach replied. "I look forward to seeing you at practice."

Ana said goodbye and then followed Cara to the library. She told Cara what had happened. Cara didn't seem very interested. For the rest of lunch, they read the comic book.

Ana checked her email and saw one from Caitlin: *How did tryouts go? Did you make it?*

Ana hesitated a moment before writing back, *Yup! I'm on the JV team. I may even be able to try pitching, like you!* It was only half a lie, and Caitlin would never know.

***

The first practice was the next day. Ana arrived early. Coach handed her a notebook that had lines, symbols, and diagrams of the softball diamond printed in it. She explained to her how to record outs, base hits, and runs for each player.

"Sometimes I'll ask you to do this during practices, but mainly it's for games," Coach told her. "First, though, can you help me carry some equipment out?"

Ana nodded. She followed coach to a supply closet and carried a big pile of gloves, masks, and bats. Some dropped to the ground while she was walking, and she had to run back along the trail of equipment to pick it all up.

This is awful, she thought.

Soon everyone else arrived to begin practicing. Laura and Mali were both there. Ana wasn't surprised to see Laura, but she had been certain that Mali would make the varsity team. She was very intense.

Coach chose one girl to lead warmups. Then everyone was divided into pairs to throw and catch. Then they started with drills.

Ana sat in the dugout with nothing to do. She didn't even have a book with her. *Everyone is having fun but me.*

CHAPTER 9

THE FIRST GAME

A few weeks later was the team's first game. Ana wore a team shirt that looked like everyone else's, except there was no number on it.

It was a home game, so the visiting team batted first. The Lions ran out to the field. Mali took her place at the pitcher's mound. Laura crouched down behind home plate. Ana sat in the dugout with her notebook. At least she would have more to do than at practice. She'd have to watch everything very carefully.

Are you coming to watch the game? she texted Cara.

A reply came quickly. *Why would I?*

Ana put her phone away. Cara hadn't been very nice lately.

The game began. Mali threw pitches hard. She struck out the first two batters. The third one hit the ball and ran to first. She was safe.

The fourth batter was a lefty. She was a powerful hitter, and she made it straight to second base while the Lions' center fielder dove for the ball and missed.

The fifth batter hit a pop up. The first baseman caught it, and it was over. Everyone jogged back to the dugout to get ready to bat.

The Lions did well. Everyone had a base hit. By the end of the inning, they were up three to nothing.

Two more innings passed. During a transition, Ana took a look at the bleachers. She gasped. Caitlin was there!

Now she'll know I lied to her. She'll probably hate me, she thought miserably.

She turned her head so Caitlin wouldn't know she had seen her. Maybe she could tell another lie and say that she was sick or injured, and that's why she wasn't playing.

At the bottom of the fourth inning, Mali struck out. She threw her bat angrily. Coach ran out to the field and called a time-out. She spoke quietly but with an angry look on her face. Mali huffed back to the dugout. She sat down far away from the rest of the team.

At the top of the fifth, Mali headed out to pitch. The first three batters all hit the ball easily. The fourth one did too, giving the other team their sixth run of the day. Now they were ahead.

Mali stamped her foot angrily. Coach called another time-out. She walked out to the field and spoke to Mali. Then the two of them walked back to the dugout together. Mali was benched!

Coach sent Shireen, the alternate, out to the field. She traded places with Marisela, the shortstop, who went to the pitcher's mound.

***

The Lions lost 13–11. As everyone packed up their things, Ana heard someone tapping at the chain-link fence. It was Caitlin.

"Hey," she said kindly. "Can I talk to you two?" She was speaking to Mali as well.

Ana and Mali both sighed and came out of the dugout. The three sat on a bleacher bench.

"Well," Caitlin said. "It seems like both of you had a bad day."

"I should've made varsity," Mali said angrily. "I hate pitching against babies. I've been playing softball my whole life."

"You're great at softball," Caitlin said. "But your attitude needs adjustment." She turned to Ana. "And why did you lie to me?"

Ana looked down so that she wouldn't have to see Caitlin's face. "I was embarrassed," she admitted. "I wanted you to be proud of me, and I'm not even playing."

"Ana, I am proud! You're new to the sport, and you're doing a really important job," Caitlin said.

"It's not the same," Ana said. "I don't matter."

"That's not true. Mali's brother is our statistician, and we really appreciate him!" Caitlin said. "His notes help us get better."

So Niran was Mali's brother! That's why Mali and her dad went to so many practices.

Caitlin sighed. "I have an idea. Mali, you have a lot of skills, and I bet you could help Ana practice. And Ana, I think your notes would be useful to Mali, and maybe you could help her with her temper. Why don't the two of you get together and practice?"

Ana and Mali looked at each other. That didn't sound so great.

CHAPTER 10

PRACTICING

Although Ana and Mali didn't want to
practice together, Mami and Mr. Kunchai agreed
with Caitlin. Soon enough, Ana found herself
at the park with Mali. After their parents dropped
them off, both girls glared at each other.

"Well," Ana said slowly. "I guess we should
get to work so we don't get in trouble again."

Mali shrugged. Both girls silently put on their
gloves. Mali pulled a softball out of her backpack.
"Think fast!" she said.

She shot the ball hard and fast. Ana jumped out of the way, letting the ball whiz past her.

"You're not going to get any better if you're afraid of the ball," Mali said. She rolled her eyes.

"I'm not afraid of the ball!" Ana yelled. "How would you like it if someone threw it at your face when you weren't ready?"

"That's what softball is!" Mali cried. "You have to be ready for everything."

"Yeah, but in a game, you're ready for it because you're watching everything," Ana said. "You're paying attention. You can anticipate where the ball is going to go after the hit and whether you're going to be a part of the play. Nobody just throws something at you for no reason."

"I didn't throw it at you for no reason. We're supposed to be practicing!" Mali insisted.

"See? You even said 'at' instead of 'to,'" Ana pointed out. "You should throw the ball *to* your teammate, not *at* them."

"Fine," Mali said. She took another softball from her bag. "Ready?" She lobbed the ball at Ana without waiting for an answer.

Ana put her glove up in a hurry. The ball bounced into her glove — and fell back out.

"Argh!" Ana cried.

"Don't hold your hand like that," Mali said.

"What do you mean?" Ana asked.

Mali jogged over to her. She showed Ana the difference between the way the two of them held their hands up when trying to catch the ball.

They tried again. This time, the ball stayed in Ana's glove. "It worked!" she said, surprised.

Mali had a few more tricks up her sleeve. She gave Ana tips on how to hold her glove for different throws and pitches. She helped Ana with her stance so that she was more steady with the bat. She even taught her how to slide into a base.

"It's not allowed in junior high sports," Mali said. "But it's fun to practice." She grinned.

Ana grinned back. It kind of hurt, but it was fun.

Later on, Mali wanted to try pitching. She handed Ana a catcher's mitt. "Use this instead of your glove," she said. "I don't have a mask, sorry."

Ana took a deep breath. She wasn't sure she wanted to catch for Mali. Her hard and fast throws looked scary. But she crouched down anyway. *I hope she goes easy on me,* she thought.

"I'll go easy to start," Mali said, as if she had read Ana's mind. Mali wound up and pitched.

Ana reached her glove up to protect her face. The ball flew right into it and knocked her back. She fell on her bottom.

"That was easy?" she shouted. But it felt kind of good. She had caught Mali's first pitch.

Mali laughed. Ana threw the ball back at her and they went again. Ana missed catching the second pitch, and for a second she saw a look of anger on Mali's face. But it quickly went away. "It's OK," Mali said. "Next time."

Ana hesitated for a moment and then said, "Hey, Mali?"

"Yeah?"

"I'm new at this, and it's a little scary when you get angry. It makes me less confident," Ana said.

Mali looked at her. "I'll try not to get so mad," she said.

Ana smiled at her.

Over time, Ana started to get used to how Mali threw the ball. Mali tilted her shoulder back for a second before winding up, and she sometimes went a little to her left. She would have to work on that so she didn't hit a left-handed batter. Ana told her that nicely. Mali's eyes flashed for a moment, but after looking at her dad, she said thank you.

By the end of the afternoon, Ana's hand hurt, but she'd had a great time. And Mali hadn't thrown anything or stomped her feet once.

CHAPTER 11

IN A PINCH

It was game day again. Everyone was suiting up in the locker room for another home game. All Ana had to do was change her shirt, so she was ready to go.

She noticed Laura sitting on a bench with her shirt changed but still wearing her jeans. She had her head in her hands. Ana went over to her.

"Are you OK, Laura?"

Laura looked up. She looked queasy. "I don't feel very well. I think I ate too much at lunch."

"Do you want some water?" Ana asked.

"I guess so," Laura said weakly.

Ana went to the watercooler and filled a paper cup. She brought it back to Laura. "Here you go."

Laura took a sip, then handed the cup back to Ana. "That's enough," she said.

"Are you going to be able to play?" asked Ana.

Laura stood up carefully. "I'm sure I'll be fine." She changed her pants and put on her cleats. Ana waited for her to make sure she was OK, and then the two of them walked out of the locker room together.

***

It was the top of the sixth inning. The other team had just made its first run, and it had runners on first and third base. Mali wound up and threw a pitch. It veered to the left, outside the batter's box. The batter didn't swing. "Ball!" called the umpire.

Mali prepared for her next pitch and let go of the ball. The batter swung. "Strike!"

Laura returned the ball to the mound, and Mali prepared for the next pitch.

"Wait!" Laura called. She got up from her crouched position and ran toward the dugout. She reached a garbage can just in time and vomited.

Coach rushed to help Laura take her gear off and led her to the bench. Ana handed Laura a cup of water.

"Thanks," Laura said in a whisper.

Coach said looked around. "I don't think you should go back out there," she said, "but Shireen's not here today." Shireen's family was observing a holiday, so she hadn't been at school all day.

"I can go back," Laura said. She began to get up off the bench and then sat down again. "No, I'm dizzy."

Coach sighed. After a moment, she asked, "Ana, have you and Mali been practicing on your own?"

"Yes!" Ana said.

"Do you think you can catch for us today?"

"Absolutely," Ana said, surprising herself with her confidence.

"OK, let's get you changed." Coach quickly explained to the umpire what was going on, and then she helped Ana into different pants and gear. Ana lumbered out to the plate.

Mali's eyes widened when she saw Ana, but she didn't say anything. The umpire looked to see that Ana was ready and then yelled, "Play ball!"

Mali wound up and pitched. It was a hit. Ana sighed with relief that she hadn't had to catch the ball, and then felt bad. *That's no good for us,* she thought.

The next batter came out. Mali struck her out. Ana caught the ball each time.

Before the seventh inning, Ana came up to Mali at the watercooler. "Hey," she said.

"Hey," said Mali. "That was a surprise."

"Listen," Ana said. "When I was watching before, I noticed something. The second batter, number 5? She swings too fast, sometimes. If you slow down your pitch, she'll probably miss it."

Mali thought for a moment. "Hmm. I'll try that. Thanks, Ana!" They ran out to the field with the rest of the Lions.

After the first batter made it to first base, number 5 came to the plate. Ana hoped Mali would remember what she said.

Mali wound up and pitched a fast one. The batter swung and missed. "Strike!"

She pitched a fast one again. The ball connected with the bat. Ana's heart sank in her stomach.

"Foul ball!" Ana ran to get the ball from the foul line.

Ana threw the ball back to Mali. *Remember! Slow!* she thought, wishing she could shout it out to Mali without the batter hearing.

Mali wound up again. And she pitched slower! As Ana expected, the batter swung fast. "Strike three!" the ump called.

The Lions cheered. Including Ana. Now she was a Lion, for real!

The next two batters hit the ball. The bases were loaded. A new batter stepped up to the plate. Mali pitched a strike, then a ball. The batter hit the third pitch, and everyone stepped into action. The first baseman caught the ball for an out.

"Home, home!" Mali cried. Ana's eyes widened. She looked at the runner coming at her. The first baseman threw the ball at her. *I have to catch this!* she thought. The ball was high. She reached her arm as far as it would go . . . and caught it.

As quickly as she could, Ana turned back to home plate. The runner was nearly there. She reached out and tagged her just before she got to the plate.

"Out!" called the umpire.

The Lions cheered. The crowd cheered. The team ran into the dugout.

At the Lions' turn to bat, they made three runs. That was all it took to win the game.

As everyone crowded back into the dugout, they shouted and shrieked and gave Ana hug after hug. "Great job, Ana!"

"Thanks for stepping in!"

Mali patted her on the back. "Welcome to the team," she said.

Ana grinned. She looked out at the bleachers and saw someone familiar. It was Caitlin! She was coming down to the dugout.

"Hey," Caitlin said. "Great job out there. I knew you could do it." Ana smiled as wide as her mouth would go.

"Thanks for your pep talk, Caitlin," she said. "Mali and I worked together."

Mali grinned at them both.

***

After she got home and told her mom the story, Ana called Cara to share it with her.

"Hello?" Cara said when she answered. She didn't sound excited to hear from her.

"Cara! I got to play!" Ana cried. "Laura got sick, which is terrible, and Shireen was gone so I got to be catcher!"

"Great."

Ana felt angry. Why wasn't Cara happier for her? Friends were supposed to be happy for one another.

"Cara?" she said. "Why aren't you excited?"

There was silence on the other end.

"Cara?" Ana repeated.

"Ever since you started softball, you've barely had time for me at all," Cara said. "You weren't excited about the comic, and you're always busy after school."

Ana thought for a moment. Instead of balancing softball with her friend, she had traded one for the other.

"You're right," she said. "I'm really sorry. How can I make it up to you?"

"Saturday," Cara said. "The new Endless Saga book is coming out. Let's go to the bookstore together to get it."

"Deal. But Cara?" Ana said.

"Yeah?"

"It really hurt my feelings when you acted like softball didn't mean anything, and you didn't want to come to the game," Ana admitted. "I'm not going to quit the team or anything."

Cara was silent for a moment. "You're right," she said. "I wasn't very nice. I don't really like sports, but if you do, I can support you."

"Thanks," Ana said, smiling. "I'll see you at school."

CHAPTER 12

A NEW SAGA

On Saturday, Ana's mom dropped her off at the mall, and she ran straight to the bookstore to meet Cara. Ana gave Cara a huge hug.

"What was that for?" Cara said with a shy smile.

"It's a thank you," Ana said. "For reminding me that I love two things equally. Playing softball with my team and being the biggest Endless Saga fan ever — with you."

Cara hugged her back.

They joined the long line to get their copies of the book. As they waited, Ana looked out the window into the mall. She saw Mali walking by with her brother. Ana waved.

Mali waved back and then, unexpectedly, she and Niran came into the bookstore. Niran smiled at Ana and said hello.

"Hi," Mali said. "What are you doing?"

"Getting our new Endless Saga books!" Ana said excitedly.

"Is that the book series about the queen and the princess battling to win a kingdom?" Mali asked.

"Yes!" Ana and Cara said at the same time. The three girls laughed.

"I've been meaning to read that," Mali said. "It sounds kind of cool."

"Stand in line with us!" Ana said. "You can buy the first book while we buy this one."

"OK," Mali said.

"Hi," Cara said to her. "I'm Cara, Ana's best friend."

"I'm Mali," Mali said. "Ana's best *softball* friend." The girls grinned at each other.

Ana put her arms around both girls. It looked like her two favorite things were about to become closer.

ABOUT the AUTHOR

Sarah Hannah Gómez has a masters of art degree in children's literature and masters of science in library science. She is now a writer and fitness instructor in Tucson, Arizona. She is working toward a doctoral degree in children's literature at the University of Arizona. Find her online at shgmclicious.com.

GLOSSARY

alternate (AWL-tur-nit)—a person who takes the place of another when necessary

concentrated (KAHN-suhn-tray-ted)—focused thoughts and attention on something

drill (DRIL)—a repeated exercise that teaches a skill or technique

honorary (ON-uh-rer-ee)—given as an honor without the usual requirements or duties

observant (ob-ZUR-vuhnt)—good at noticing things

passionate (PASH-uh-nit)—having or showing very strong feelings

precision (pri-SIZH-uhn)—the quality or state of being very accurate or exact

recruited (RI-KROOT-ed)—worked to get an athlete to join a certain team

statistician (stat-i-STISH-uhn)—a person who records and tracks a team's numerical information, for example batting averages

technique (tek-NEEK)—a method or way of doing something that requires skill

unison (YOO-nuh-suhn)—the state of two or more people doing something together

DISCUSSION QUESTIONS

1. What specific things led to Ana's interest
   in softball? Have you ever experienced a
   similar new and sudden interest in a sport
   or hobby? Compare your experience with
   Ana's.

2. Explain why Ana chose to lie to Caitlin
   about making the team. How would the
   story have been different if she had not been
   caught in her lie?

3. Ana's and Cara's friendship hit a rough
   patch. What or who was mainly responsible
   for this? Use evidence from the book to
   support your answer. Have you ever
   experienced something similar?

WRITING PROMPTS

1. Revisit the team tryouts in Chapter 6. Now rewrite the tryouts in first person from Ana's point of view. Be sure to tap into her senses, as well as her thougths and feelings.

2. You are a sportswriter! Write a newspaper story covering the Lions' game at the end of the book.

3. Compare and contrast Ana, Mali, and Cara. Write about how they are similar, and how they differ.

SOFTBALL
AROUND THE WORLD

The United States is known for softball, but it's played in other countries too. Learn all about it!

From 1996 to 2008, softball was a sport in the Summer Olympics. Thirteen countries, including the United States, sent teams over the years. It will return to the Olympics for the Summer 2020 games in Tokyo.

The World Cup of Softball is hosted by the Amateur Softball Association in Oklahoma. Eight different countries have participated, including the United States.

The International Softball Federation governs women's and men's softball leagues. There are 124 member countries, including the United States, from six continents.

In 2004, Japanese softball player Yukiko Ueno pitched the first perfect game in Olympic history.

Softball was introduced to Australia in 1939 as a school sport.

In the women's league of the Costa Rica Softball Association, women of all ages participate, even 60 years and older!

Oria Wood Knowles' softball career in the Bahamas lasted 34 years.

Softball is called by its English name in most languages. However, in Maori it is called *poiuka*, in Afrikaans it is called *sagtebal*, and in Welsh it is called *pêl feddal*.